A Little Bit Of What You Fanc'

A Little Bit Of W...

A Short Story Collection (Vol 1)

By David Ellis

Acknowledgement

This collection would not have been possible without the friendship, support and encouragement that I have received from my local creative writing group The Tunbridge Wells & District Writers' Circle.

I have had the honour to meet some very talented individuals who have inspired me to treat my writing very seriously. I sincerely hope that they all manage to get their words in print for the world to see because when they do, what a glorious place it will be.

I would like to therefore make a special shout out to the following individuals who have been hugely influential in my writing life and have encouraged me time and time again to put pen to pad and fingers to keyboard. I am humbled to know many creative and talented individuals and these people have a special place in my heart.

A Little Bit Of What You Fancy - A Short Story Collection

Caroline Auckland

Margaret Hazell-Smith

Sarah Heath

Amanda Lynch

Clare Marsh

Lesley McCall

Karen Rollason

Alby Stockley

Jacquie Wyatt

Furthermore, I have another group of people who greatly inspired me during my tenure at The Tunbridge Wells Writers' Circle. I've mentioned them separately to highlight their published written works and where to find them.

David Barry – David has many novels in print and on Amazon Kindle. His author website can be found at:-

http://www.davidbarryauthor.co.uk

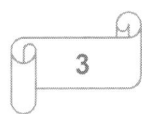

A Little Bit Of What You Fancy - A Short Story Collection

Anna Cullum – Anna has a collection of Short Stories on Amazon Kindle called 'Floripa Shorts'.

Anna Faversham – Anna has novels on Amazon Kindle in the time slip romantic fiction genre, most notably 'Hide In Time' and 'One Dark Night'.

Justin Hamlin – Justin has three novels on Amazon Kindle in the urban fantasy and crime thriller/horror genres including a selection of Short Stories called 'Dogmeat'. His novels are 'Jezebel' & 'The Samurai of Gosford Green'.

Hilary Mackelden – Hilary has several novels that have been published and writes plays, pantomimes and screenplays.

Her website can be found at

http://www.hilarymackelden.com

A Little Bit Of What You Fancy - A Short Story Collection

Angela McPherson – Angela publishes under the name of Verity Short. She has two novels available in paperback and on Amazon Kindle titled 'Norah & Emma' and 'The Alice Band'.

Michael Robertson – Michael has published many novels on Amazon Kindle in the post-apocalyptic genre.

His website can be found at www.michalrobertson.co.uk

Finally, I would like to sincerely thank my brother Declan Ellis for helping me with formatting issues and website creation issues, he is a technical guru and his knowledge knows no bounds. I also believe that he cannot be killed by conventional weapons.

A Little Bit Of What You Fancy - A Short Story Collection

Cover design by David Ellis (Cover Photo by Ryan McGuire at www.gratisography.com)

Copyright © 2016 by David Ellis. 3rd Edition.

Publisher – CreateSpace Publishing.

All rights reserved. No part of this publication may be reproduced, distributed, or transmitted in any form or by any means, including photocopying, recording, or other electronic or mechanical methods, without the prior written permission of the publisher, except in the case of brief quotations embodied in critical reviews and certain other non-commercial uses permitted by copyright law.

For permission requests, write to the author at the e-mail address provided in the 'About the Author' page.

Please support the author by reviewing this book on Amazon, Goodreads and Barnes & Noble.

A Little Bit Of What You Fancy - A Short Story Collection

Foreword

I hope that you enjoy the Short Stories in this collection, I have been often told that there are many of them that could be expanded upon and I intend to do this with some of them in the near future. The first half of the book contains Flash Fiction pieces that were submitted to competitions and highly praised at the time of their creation. The second half of the book contains Short Stories that have been published in my local newspaper and commercially published in Amazon Kindle anthologies.

My award winning debut poetry collection is now also available and can be purchased on Amazon Kindle or in print – it is called 'Life, Sex & Death – A Poetry Collection (Vol 1)'.

My Twitter handle is @TooFullToWrite and my website can be found at www.toofulltowrite.com

Thank you for reading and keep watching the skies.

About the Author

David Ellis is an award winning poet and author of poetry, fiction and music lyrics.

His debut poetry collection 'Life, Sex & Death' won an International Award in the Readers' Favorite Book Awards 2016 for Inspirational Poetry Books.

He lives in Tunbridge Wells, Kent in the UK.

David is extremely fond of cats and dogs but not snakes.

Indiana Jones is his spirit animal.

He can be contacted at davidellisbusiness@gmail.com.

A Little Bit Of What You Fancy - A Short Story Collection

Contents

A Little Bit Of What You Fancy 1
Acknowledgement 2
Foreword 7
Part 1 – With Flash Fiction, You Can Do Anything But Not Everything 11
    Colour It In 12
    Art On The Run 14
    Searching For Paradise Lost 17
    Sweet Merciful Release 19
    The Healing Process 22
    A Familiar Itch 25
    Junior's First Words 28
    10 Things The Boss Hates About Me 33
    A Successful Succession Of Snafus 39
    Next Year's Resolutions 44
    No End In Sight 49
    Sentimental Value 53
    Beating Them At Their Own Game 57
    Elementary My Dear, Watkins 61
    Give The Lad An Oscar 67
    Losing The Plot 70
    A Little Bit Of What You Fancy 75
    Our Utopia 80
    Think Before Choosing Pink 83
    Traditional Reservations 86

Dodging The Issue 90

Give Peace A Chance 93

A Family Of Marionettes 95

Fiddling While Rome Burns To A Different Tune 98

A Ghost Of A Chance 101

Part 2 - Right In The Shorts! **104**

Cherry Picking The Winner 105

Prelude To Getting Led Out 111

Night-Bloomer 117

Time Outside the Cage 124

A Magical Tale Of 'The Dazzling Davido' 132

A Blast From The Past 135

A Little Bit Of What You Fancy - A Short Story Collection

Part 1 – With Flash Fiction, You Can Do Anything But Not Everything

A Little Bit Of What You Fancy - A Short Story Collection

Colour It In

There is a story that rips across the very fabric of time and space.

Of rainbows that leave their scars across the mind's eye of the sky.

Sometimes the world grows up to listen to this story.

Sometimes the story is ignored.

But the story is a living, breathing, beast of a thing.

It bucks and thrusts and changes with the wind, changes in a heartbeat.

It consumes those who do not respect its power, strikes fear into the hearts of mortal man/woman and sends electricity down the spines and souls that it consumes.

Sometimes you can dine on its opulence with the starkest clarity you have ever experienced in your life.

Sometimes you can wallow in the pity, self-loathing and gnarlment of discovery that it puts you through.

But if you give it time, let it creep insidiously into your life, filling your lungs with the joy, fear, hope and wonderment that it can bring, you can indulge in a power that is stronger than the love of a thousand lifetimes.

You just have to let the right one into your life and everything changes.

Sometimes for the better, sometimes for the worse but always for the greater good of your being.

Art On The Run

It's been five years since the accident that robbed me of my sight. Funny how when you lose one particular sense, time slows down and all of your remaining senses are heightened to razor like sharpness.

Some people sow seeds, others dig roads. Me? I was, am and will always be an artist. I work with shapes and navigate by the touch of objects.

It wasn't always like this.

I used to paint, to sculpt, to control the very world in my hands and conjure up beauty at my fingertips at every opportunity. That's when I met Judith, who shared my artistic flair and passions. For us, art was a means to communicate and a way to flirt with each other, which ultimately drew us closer together.

A Little Bit Of What You Fancy - A Short Story Collection

    We were passionate lovers, sharing a kaleidoscope of colours. We would paint oceans, landscapes and magical fortresses together, our collective experience moving us so emotionally that we held hands together while we painted.

Some mornings she would swim in and out of focus, as if some nefarious character were spinning the lenses on my telescope. But I never told her, I kept this secret to myself and she could tell that something was terribly wrong.

    I kept picking apart our relationship, all this noise, fear, guilt and anxiety. All I could think about was the terrible burden that I would put on her if she stayed and as I gradually began to lose all semblance of my vision, I became the blind man running, always running from my one true love.

She would have stayed by my side but I deliberately broke her heart and now she'll never know how I truly feel. Sometimes I stare out into the abyss, teeter tottering over the edge, embracing the darkness to experience one last sporadic fleeting glance of light. Where every misstep is fraught with danger and becomes an adventure in your own mind.

Love, just like art will always find a way, you just have to learn to embrace it.

Come back to me Judith. Only you can make me whole again.

Searching For Paradise Lost

It was the ring.

I had been ignoring all the other signs at first but this had been the clincher. I needed a drink. Something strong to cut through the pain.

To think, less than five hours ago, I was struggling to find a babysitter for Beth & Tommy. Sometimes you question what pitfalls and pratfalls you are going to encounter when you are raising a family alone because the deadbeat Dad takes off with some young strumpet half his age.

Dammit, I needed at least two drinks to take the edge off and that's a lot for someone who doesn't drink that often. I'd let my hair down once a month with the girls from the hotel that I clean at.

Never met a man at one of these "sinfests" (as Julie at work likes to call them) and then somebody had the bright idea to tell me to go speed-dating.

"It's lame, I don't want to go!" I lamented but I knew that arguing with the girls was not going to get me anywhere, such was their will and strong resolve. They kept me on track through the divorce, that's why they were my friends.

God, I had missed her for so long, I had pretty much given up hope in finding her. But I never forgot the Butterfly signet ring Daddy gave her – now that I've found her again, I'm never letting her go.

Then the bell goes and I'm alone again, forever.

Damn you, Mother.

Sweet Merciful Release

Clint had tried everything.

"How do you turn this damn thing off?"

He had tried counting sheep.

Drinking copious amounts of alcohol (that just gave him a searing headache).

Washing the dishes (he'd had to make them dirty again several times, as he only ever had a few items to wash up in the sparse flat that he dared to call his 'abode').

Counting the ceiling tiles (1217 of them. He had double and triple checked for good measure).

Listening to music – he had tried pop, jazz, funk, soul, classical, easy listening, even Egyptian Death Metal. None of them helped send him on his journey with Mr Sandman into the land of nod.

Reading – this was the worst of all, he kept getting too far into the plot and wanting to read more. Why was the dragon hoarding all of the gold? How many dusky maidens were going to be sacrificed before the hero did anything? Why is there a bard skipping around the town in purple pajamas infecting everyone with his insidious song?

"Argh! – This stupid novel is making my brain somersault into overdrive!" Clint lamented sorrowfully.

Writing – he'd managed his shopping list and the lyrics to some half formed song in his head but that kept getting broadsided by someone with a very big shouty voice thundering "Insomniomniomnia!"

He tried reading the dictionary and that didn't make him tired, just deeply bored, frustrated and with an urgent need to smash something to smithereens.

Scented candles didn't work either. He'd tried buying one of those massive joss stick things that smelt like perfumed bacon to see if that would dull his twitching senses but this too had been ineffectual and given him sinus trouble.

He'd tried acupuncture, aromatherapy, homeopathy, psychotherapy, electric shock treatment, hypnotherapy and even staring at the wall in the past but he might as well be hitting the Eiffel tower with a teaspoon.

Yet every day at four in the morning, his head would sink into the pillow and his brain would temporarily switch off from the creative stimuli driving him on its juggernautesque journey every bleeding night without fail just like it had always done for the last thirteen years.

"This is the price that you pay for creativity but I pay it gladly" He thought.

And with that, at exactly the stroke of midnight, he started his 52nd opera with a dutiful exuberance.

The Healing Process

Why is everything so damn foggy? Where are my glasses? Can't remember what I was reading last night.

Damn cockroaches. I'd flatten them but this place is dirty enough as it is.

My Daddy was a Doctor. Or a Fireman. Maybe a Newscaster. I don't know.

The first guess was probably right.

There's a phrase that keeps on recurring in my mind, might be French or Greek or something – "**Similia similibus curantur**" – Daddy used to use fancy words a lot, said it meant something about "Like curing like."

I'll drink to that. Poison the well a little more.

Can't remember when I last ate, might have been a hamburger, I can see the wrapper on the floor.

Can still smell the onions. Are they green? Must be at least a couple of days old. What's wrong with me? How'd it get so bad my only friend in the world is a bottle of moonshine? But nothing shines in this dump unless it's swimming in grease.

Another object swims into focus. There are words. A newspaper. Open on the obituaries section.

Oh Lordy, I've missed Daddy's funeral! I'm a terrible son, I know I need to do better, I…wait, what day is it today? Is it a Tuesday?

I missed his funeral over three years ago.

Guess I have been a little preoccupied lately, what with…what was it now?

Oh yeah, Lucy Lou dying too.

I loved her. Best darn mutt there ever was.

Bottle's almost empty now, might as well just be guzzling on tears. Seems everything I hold dear has run its course, expired, left me.

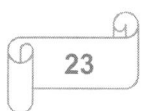

But my sister is coming over today I think – or it may be next week.

    Don't know. Don't really care.

She's bringing a suit, has told me to clean my act up.

    "Do it for your niece!" She shrieked.

I can barely tie my own shoelaces nowadays.

    Maybe I'll just sleep here for a while.

If they turn up, I'll pretend I'm out.

    Wouldn't be the first time.

A Familiar Itch

"Patchy. And it makes me itch like a son of a...."

"Now William, that is not language becoming of a young gentleman! All of the men in our distinguished lineage sport perfectly groomed moustaches. How else can we effectively convey to the masses the austerity of our honourable name without good manners, fine looking clothes and immaculately coiffured facial hair?"

"I'm not sure I want all of this Mother." William waved his hand dismissively at the manor.

"Nonsense, what would you do if you aren't going to take over the family business?"

"I'd quite like to work with my pal Derek." William looked pleadingly at his Mother.

Penelope screwed up her fizzog in barely contained contempt.

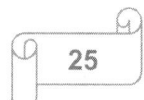

"Derek? Isn't he the grubby little oik who works in that ghastly hardware store in the more "obnoxious" area of this district?"

"That hardware store is a family business that has been running for the last 21 years Mother!"

"And your own family business has been running for five times longer than that and yet you wish to flagrantly throw it away at the behest of your 'friend' who you've only know for a few months."

"Two years and several months actually Mother."

"Hush, tish and pishaw William, don't contradict your Mother. The fact of the matter is that Derek is not your family and you are heir to our name and I simply will not allow you to squander this opportunity. I expressively forbid you to associate with Derek anymore."

"You're too late, I've signed a contact."

Penelope's jaw dropped so low that the devil himself could have heard it knocking on the gates of hell.

"William! How could you besmirch the family name like this! And me, your Mother. This business is our bread and butter. Your Father has been taken ill for quite some time now, you must forget all this nonsense and stop taking leave of your senses."

"Give the business to the butler Mother, I hear that he is keen to get stuck in."

"I will disown you William, you can count on it!"

"I'd rather be free Mother than your puppet!"

And with that William ran out.

But his Mother bought the business from Derek's father the next day and then fired William.

Because it's a family business and you can't fight the familiar itch.

Junior's First Words

"Turn the TV set off – your son is trying to talk to you!"

"I don't speak baby babble kitten. Plus, I'm missing the game. Pass me another brew would you darlin'?"

"Hello?" She waved frantically in front of his face, causing him to grunt in consternation. "I asked you a question Joe – how old do you think your son is?"

"I dunno. You know I ain't good at math cupcake. At least one?"

"He's two and a half – Jeez Louise! It's like you spend your whole life watching that damn TV set."

"That's not true Isabelle. Why, take last week for example when I mowed the lawn…"

"Huh yeah, for about the first time in over three years and that's only 'cos I made your fat, lazy ass do it 'cos my Mommy & Daddy were coming round."

"Baby, I can't be tied down. I'm a free spirit, y'know?"

"I can see plenty of free spirit alright, being suckled down your gullet in Jack and Cokes."

Joe sighed and switched off the TV set.

"OK then, you win cherry pie. Let's see what Junior has to say for himself."

"He nearly said his first word yesterday."

"He's moved beyond 'bluuglefloobitydooperdurgle'? That's progress I guess."

"Do you even care about your son's development? If you took an interest, he could be a doctor. A musician. A scientollorolloragist."

"Careful with the big words Izzy darlin' – don't want to be doing yourself an injury there pancake."

She stood up and put two fingers of each hand in the air like quotation marks

"Huh, well I'm sorry 'Professor' – I'm surprised you have a brain at all, I thought watching too much TV could make you dumber than a box of chocolates dropped at an old people's home."

Joe danced Junior on his leg and Junior giggled.

"Sounds like Mommy is in a real bad mood Junior – do you think she wants a hug?"

Junior shrugged then tried to squirm off Joe's knee.

"I need more than just a hug. I need you to start doing something with your life and set a good example for Junior."

"What brought all this on?"

She bit her lip. "I'm pregnant again Joe."

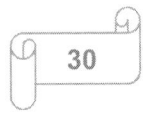

The bottom had just fallen out of Joe's world.

"You're sure you have another bun in the oven Sweet Pea?

He really wished he had told her about the snip just after Junior's birth. But the time had never been right.

Hell, they didn't get that intimate often anyway.

And now their family was going to have to live with more than one secret.

"This is the happiest day of my life." Joe's stomach knotted as he uttered these words but he showed nothing but elation to Isabelle.

"Oh do you really mean it Joe?" Isabelle hugged him.

"Yes I do."

But he didn't.

As Isabelle sauntered off humming happily into the kitchen, Joe poured himself another generous measure of Jack and Coke then turned to Junior.

"Here's to the future…." He raised his glass to Junior's inquisitive stare.

"Burblebooyukyuk…Daddy!"

"You said it kid – you said it."

10 Things The Boss Hates About Me

"I'm late."

"I'm always late."

Donald tousled his sweat drenched hair, creating a side parting you could have parked a Sherman tank in. He untucked his shirt a little, letting in a bit of cool air to circulate around his ample frame and fanned himself with a magazine.

The office Christmas party had bled and segued into the early hours of the morning.

Major Account meeting?

Major 'In dire need of a hangover cure' more like it.

Percy from Accounts (or 'That Pillock, a nice guy but a complete tool all the same' as Donald affectionately refers to him behind his back) had kept him out drinking all night, not really against his will but still an undesirable anchor to excess all the same.

"Why do I always put myself into these stressful situations, leaving everything until the last minute – I'm so disorganised!" Donald's thoughts raced around his head like the last lap of a neurological grand prix.

Hastily stuffing a pack of Monster Munch crisps into his mouth (Pickled Onion – what was he thinking?), Donald barely made it to his interconnecting train by the skin of his teeth.

"I wish I'd bought some deodorant." Donald mused to himself, as his fellow passengers winced at an unholy odour billowing from him, akin to a particularly fragrant kitty litter tray filling their reluctant nostrils. He put his hand to his mouth, breathing hard. "Ruddy hellfire – I could do with some breath mints too!"

Running from the underground station at a pace that could no less be described as breakneck (which he almost did on at least two occasions), he took the steps to the client's office two at a time and tried to compose himself, as he made his way to the entrance past the obliging receptionist.

The presentation didn't go well at all.

Being several minutes late, extremely flustered and red-faced is hardly an encouraging sign for potential investors at the best of times.

Dejectedly taking off after acknowledging their 'Don't call us, we'll call you polite smiles and mannerisms', Donald crawled into the nearest bar he could find in search of liquid refreshment.

Sinking a couple of cheeky cocktails, he was approached by an inquisitive stranger, who bought him another drink.

"I'm Rupert." He held out his hand to Donald expectantly.

"Donald." They shook hands briskly, Donald's palms were still a bit squidgy from earlier.

Gulping from his whiskey glass and spying the finished drinks around them, Rupert nodded at Donald.

"You look like you've been through quite an ordeal today Donald – care to share your story with this old war horse?"

Donald opened up the floodgates with unrestrained gusto, filling Rupert in on every detail of the terrible fiasco of a meeting and a lot more, thanks to alcohol greasing the conversation wheels.

"I'm a walking advertisement for everything that bosses hate." Donald held up his drink in one hand and started counting on the other in front of Rupert.

"I'm smelly, late, unreliable, a bully (but then everybody bullies Percy the Pillock at my office), I won't admit to mistakes, I'm a bit of a gossip, never satisfied with my lot in life, hate change and wish things would remain the same, often deal with personal stuff at work and don't do enough to reduce my bosses' workload. A real bonafide hero to my kids, if I had any."

Donald drained his martini glass and started to walk away from Rupert, their conversation coming to a close.

"So what's going to happen to you Donald – will you get some grief or static back at the office?"

"Nah, I'll be alright."

"You didn't tell me the name of your company?"

Donald handed Rupert his card, shook his hand, said "Look me up online friend" and then left.

Rupert peered at it and read 'Donald Jacobson's Emporium – Owner'.

Rupert finished his whiskey, moved the press pass in his bag aside and stared at the pad of paper with the article he was writing – 'The Decline of the British Empire and How We Need More Entrepreneurs'.

Screwing up the article in disgust, Rupert hurled it in the bin and stared despondently out the window.

"I'm going to miss my deadline again." Rupert continued to mutter into his whiskey.

"I'm going to be late." "I'm always late…"

A Successful Succession Of Snafus

Julia could tell from a mile off that this was going to be a long day.

A loooooooooooong day.

She had already put salt in her coffee, sugar on her poached eggs and both her son Albert and hubby Dale were going to get nice little surprises when they opened their lunch bags. Albert; a beef and horseradish sauce doorstep cut loaf that would be far too big for his tiny chompers to cope with and for Dale; a smattering of cute tessellated cheese triangle sandwiches.

If hubby makes it out of work alive under the sheer weight of embarrassment, he's going to be mighty hungry when he gets back – I'll have to make it up to him.

Julia's thoughts turned to a soothing glass of wine, as she switched on to autopilot, taking care of the household chores.

However, she was so distracted by the drama unfolding on the Jeremy Kyle show about fathers who cheat on their partners with other fathers called Eric, she nearly poured herself a glass of vinegar instead.

Ironic how some of these cheaper whites taste like they would be better served over fish and chips anyway.

Julia then gazed down at the washing machine and screamed.

"Oh no – hubby's clothes have been washing at the wrong temperature!"

She tapped her foot impatiently, waiting for the washing machine to finish draining off its cycle after she violently jabbed the cancellation button.

Well, I guess my little Albert could wear hubby's clothes, now that they're probably ten sizes too small for him.

Lady Luck was not smiling on Julia today.

In between a power cut and then subsequently burning the roast dinner she had lovingly prepared for Dale to make up for her lunch faux pas earlier, Julia began to feel as if she could do nothing right.

She decided she was going to make herself look really nice for Dale and enjoy some quality time with him tonight – there was no way she was going to screw this up!

Julia put Albert to bed and then headed into the bathroom. As she dove into the shower, she missed the telephone, which went to the answerphone after several rings.

When she had finished washing herself, she tied her hair up into a bun, did her nails, slipped into a silky robe and chuckling to herself, slipped a rose between her teeth. Dale would be impressed!

The doorbell rang and she rushed down to answer it breathlessly.

"Hey there handsom....uhh?"

Dale was there holding some flowers behinds his Mother Dorris.

Out of the corner of her eye, she saw the answering machine light flashing accusingly.

Dorris gave her daughter-in-law a quizzical glance. "Why are you in a dressing gown dear, are you not well?"

Dorris spotted the rose clenched between Julia's teeth. Realisation dawned.

"Oh! Somebody's getting lucky tonight!" Dorris winked mischievously "And I don't mean on the lottery! Give me five!"

Dorris held her hand out expectantly at her son.

"Come on, don't leave me hanging!"

Dale sheepishly smacked his Mother's hand; Dorris then wandered past them into the kitchen, whistling to herself while Dale mustered up the courage to look at Julia.

Julia bit down hard on the rose, nearly severing the head clean off. Her fierce glare transmitted the message loud and clear to her husband —*This is going to take one hell of a back rub and a ginormous glass of wine to fix, let me tell you!*

Dale swallowed nervously.

"Guess I had better not tell you about my day at the office then?"

Dale was not a stupid man, he knew when to zip it, the secret as to why their marriage had lasted over twenty years.

She softened and embraced him.

"Is your Mother staying long?"

"About as long as it took me to eat those cheese sandwiches!"

They both grinned devilishly at each other. It would appear that something was finally going to go right today after all.

Next Year's Resolutions

Tom and Jeremy plonked themselves down on the sofa, clutching the brows of their aching noggins, still suffering from their hangovers from the previous night's New Year Celebration revelry.

Tom however looked very pleased with himself.

"The problem with most people nowadays Jeremy is that they set themselves tasks that are impossible to achieve. Everyone has their limits and they have to make achievable goals to reflect this. Take drinking for example…"

Jeremy interrupted irritably – "Ah yes, booze. God my head hurts. Since it's a New Year and a fresh new start, what kind of resolution are you going to make about the demon drink?"

"Well I'm going to drink less. And when I say drink less, I mean less wine. The occasional beer isn't really drinking, especially if it's after work or with a meal. And since I tend to drink more red than say white or Rosé, I think I will reduce my red intake and have the odd glass of white/Rosé instead."

"Isn't that robbing Peter to pay Paul?"

"Not from where I'm standing. Hell, it's practically healthy!"

"How do you mean exactly Tom?"

"Well Jeremy…" Tom unfolded his arms and started to gesticulate like he was a college professor illustrating a particularly tricky mathematical theory to an avid pupil.

"They say that you can clear up a red wine stain off the sofa if you pour white wine on it." Tom beamed triumphantly.

"So?" Jeremy looked both puzzled and indignant, which gave him the air and grace of someone with mild constipation.

Tom looked at him haughtily like he was ever so slightly thick.

"So my dear Jeremy, imagine the good it will do my body – might clean me pipes out a treat."

"That's hogwash Tom but I see no point in arguing the point with you – what other resolutions have you got up your sleeves?"

"I'm also going to eat less chocolate."

"But you hardly ever eat chocolate Tom, you eat biscuits instead."

"Exactly. Achievable. I can't lose!"

"But the biscuits that you eat have chocolate on them!"

"Not as much chocolate as you find in an actual bar of chocolate though – everything in moderation." Tom tapped his nose knowingly.

Jeremy threw his hands up in exasperation.

"OK, fine, what about exercise? Are you going to make a resolution for that then?"

"Yes I did, I thought of going to the gym. But I had another resolution where I wanted to save more money and spend less therefore I'm going to exercise at home."

"I've never ever seen you do a push-up or a sit-up."

"Well I walk to the shops don't I? That has to count. I'll just take the scenic route instead."

"Which is what?"

"Well if I walk down the road instead of up, that should significantly increase the number of steps that I take."

"To a shop where you are buying booze and biscuits."

"That's not fair Jeremy." Tom pouted. "Sometimes I buy milk too."

"So your resolutions are to drink ever so slightly less...red wine, to exercise ever so slightly more and to eat less of a junk food that you don't particularly partake much of in the first place?"

"That's about the size of it."

"Well I have to admit that sounds very achievable – I'll drink to that."

"Me too – pub?"

"Sounds good – while we're there, we can start to think about Next Year's Resolutions!"

No End In Sight

She was all up in his grill.

He could feel her hot breath, as she moved in closer and closer.

He felt her invading his personal space in the same creepy familiar way that she always reserved for these encounters but right now there was nothing he could do about.

He was helpless, powerless, rooted to the spot.

Click.

Click click.

It took him all of his considerable willpower not to snigger in her face.

He knew that such insolence would not go down well and he would possibly be punished for this behaviour. The ritual however was so bizarre that the absurdity of it all made him want to throw caution to the wind and allow himself the luxury of a surreptitious guffaw.

Focusing harder in the ghoulish semi-darkness and attempting not to look directly at her, he began pretending that she was a snake headed viperous Medusa but in spite of these efforts, his eyes were inevitably drawn magnetically back to her commanding presence.

"Look at me Hector! Look at me!" She clicked her fingers at him impatiently.

Hector reluctantly complied with the request.

"That's good, there's a good little boy."

She had blown in his eye earlier.

Right in the socket.

It had made him very uncomfortable and he had heroically fought the urge to weep.

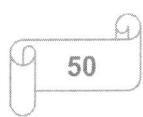

But he had to tough his way through this. He was a man. And real men don't cry. Real men bleed and bury their feelings. His mind began to wander. He wondered if he was strong enough to endure this torture.

As time dragged on, she made things even more uncomfortable for him. His vision had begun to blur and she continued to encourage this further.

More questions. More clicking. More gadgets and devices to cause him distress and discomfort.

But nothing could prepare him for the final question she posed:-

"Green or red?"

"I don't know."

"Come on Hector, you can tell me and this will all be over soon."

"Green or red?"

It's a trick! "Neither!" he replied smugly.

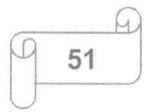

"OK then, everything still seems to be the same. I guess you're free to go."

Hector made a run for it and then stumbled out into the light outside, blinking furiously.

Hector had made it out of there this time with everything intact but next time, he might not be so lucky.

A woman approached him at the entrance of the building.

"How did it go? No glasses?"

Hector shook his head.

And with that he took his Mother's hand and they headed off home.

Sentimental Value

The walls were bleeding now.

Shedding their viscous tears without a care in the world.

"Another biscuit to go with your cup of Earl Grey Officer?" She twinkled and wrinkled her nose towards the policeman.

"Thank you Mrs Greene, very kind of you."

"Sally."

"Thank you Sally – I do like the ones with cream in the middle."

"They're my favourite too."

Officer Hadron supped his tea noisily, savouring every drop like his life depended on it. He picked up his notebook and thumbed through the pages, licking his fingers occasionally.

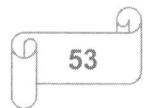

"We've had reports off things going missing in the area Sally. Knick-knacks mostly."

"Knick-knacks officer?" Sally's voice was politely inquisitive as she glanced at the wall again, which was now becoming a darker shade of red and oozing like a sticky, gooey river of syrup.

"Curios Ms Greene…Sally. Antiques. Watches, brooches, rings, necklaces. Items of great sentimental value."

"Oh yes, I understand."

Officer Hadron peered carefully over the top of his glasses at her in an appraising matter.

Seems like a bit of a daft old bat, like she's away with the fairies half the time, he thought to himself.

"Well we don't want to take up too much of your valuable time Sally, we just wanted to inquire if you had heard anything or seen anything suspicious?"

"Mmmmmm me? Oh no, nothing at all."

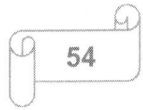

The wall was threatening to explode all over them in a geyser, spraying them both with the fetid stench of guilt.

"Is something the matter Sally?"

"Oh no Officer, I'm just thinking about my son, he's been away for so long."

"Is he in the army?"

"No, he's gone overseas with his girlfriend."

"So you're here on your own?"

"I manage Officer, I have few possessions of value in my humble abode, I imagine I will be perfectly safe from this crazy kleptomaniac you speak of."

"Well if you hear of anything then here's my card, give me a call, it could be very important."

"Thank you Officer, let me see you out."

Officer Hadron picked up his hat and headed for the door.

"When will your son be back? I suspect you miss him dearly?"

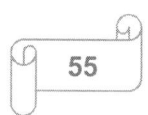

"Oh I do Officer, I do but I always feel as if part of him is here with me and will be forever."

She stared at her slippers and noticed that there was a red patch on them. Officer Hadron looked at them and caught her gaze.

"Dropped a bit of strawberry cheesecake on them!"

Officer Hadron shrugged and left.

"Good one Mum!" said Nathan from behind the wall cavity.

"Shut up Nathan – you only have sentimental value to me now, unlike that stuff you stole. I hope it keeps you happy in there!"

And with that she went to get more cheesecake from the fridge.

Beating Them At Their Own Game

"Every time I go on holiday they rip me off, my wallet always gets pinched, everyone is a potential thief. They all steal from me. Not today!"

Jacob was going to be ready this time round.

Last time on his hols, a young hooligan had pretended to be drunk, kicked off an argument with a few people, then bumped into him, before apologising, running off with a far steadier gait of someone who wasn't really drunk at all but who had certainly appeared to be at the time and half-inched his wallet.

(What's the world coming to when you can't trust a young hooligan to be drunk or even mildly inebriated? They were a better class of hooligan in my day; they certainly knew how to disrespect their elders, let me tell you).

Jacob whipped out his spare credit card he had for emergencies, bought a replacement wallet and then twenty seconds later, another young ruffian had spilt milk on him. They cleaned it off, then quickly cleared off and he'd been cleaned out again – somebody was milking it, that's for sure but they would have been sour to learn nothing was in there.

"A small victory but a victory none the less I suppose." He mused.

This gave Jacob an idea – *"Why don't I beat them at their own game!"*

He carefully wrote a list on the back of his grocery shopping list (because he liked to recycle):-

1. Plastic whistle in case I'm attacked (don't want to set any airport metal detectors off).

2. Bun bag for my wallet, strapped to my back, with a small padlock.

3. Spare cash cellotaped to my leg under my sock (another good place is in my boxers that I'm wearing. In the front not the back of course, I'm not a drug mule).

4. A cheap, disposable mobile phone.

5. The Encyclopaedia Britannica (in case I need to look anything up because my cheap mobile doesn't get the internet).

6. A helmet to prevent my bonce being bashed in if I am mugged. I can wear it all the time on holiday and pretend I'm a cyclist.

7. A fake Kindle (not for any reason other than for my own amusement if it's stolen).

8. My camera in a large, elegant cake box. Smeared in cake. Then any would be thieves will think it is a camera cake. "The camera never lies." Oh, the irony!

9. Bulky bicycle chain – might as well hire out a bike, I will be wearing a helmet all the time.

10. Various assorted Styrofoam balls, rags and other soft objects to keep everything from bashing about in transit.

He had thought of everything – he felt like a genius. "At last – finished!" He exclaimed, his suitcase now virtually bulging and stuffed to the gills. Nothing had been left to chance – no-one was going to get the better of him this time.

"*Now…*" Jacob pondered thoughtfully, *"where am I meant to fit all my clothes…."*

Elementary My Dear, Watkins

Larry straightened his tie and frowned at himself in the mirror.

"These Windsor knots are a pain in the ar…."

"Larry! Watch your language around Monique please!"

"I was going to say arms, honey!"

Larry smiled at Jessica – she knew she couldn't get mad at him. He was a brave, good, kind, sensitive man and she loved him dearly.

It was Larry's first new day as a teacher at Watkins Elementary School. The only fires he would be fighting now would be in the hearth of his own front living room.

All he had ever known was being a fireman. His Dad had been a fireman and his Father had also been a fireman before him. But he knew he had to make the change. For the sake of his family and for his own health, after much soul searching, he decided that teaching was the way forward. He had been doing a home study course for the past few months and now he felt the time was right to take the plunge.

Jessica gave his hand a reassuring squeeze.

"You'll be great Larry, just you wait and see."

Larry grabbed Jessica and kissed her passionately, eliciting a groan at knee height.

"Sheesh, get a room you two lovebirds!"

"Don't you worry Monique, I'll get my revenge when you start chasing boys! In fact, I may end up chasing them too – straight out the hallway and down the road if they're not suitable!"

Monique blew her tongue out at her Father and raced out the door for school.

"It's a good thing that she doesn't go to Watkins – I see enough of her every day as it is."

"I know you're teasing Larry. It's a shame that she doesn't though, since she doesn't know anyone at her new school. I'm sure that will change at some point in the near future. Anyway, stop stalling now or you'll be late for class – go and show them what you're made of!"

Larry kissed Jessica on the cheek and headed off to his car.

The drive was fairly uneventful, except for a rogue squirrel that nearly caused him to flip his vehicle like The Dukes of Hazzard. This did his already jangling nerves no good at all but as he drove closer to Watkins, he thought of Jessica and the faith that she had instilled in him, which gave him serenity and confidence.

As he pulled up into his parking space, he noticed a young boy weeping by the side of the road.

"Larry jumped out of his car and sat by the boy.

"Few things in life are worth crying about son. Why so sad?"

The boy looked up.

"Didn't you used to be a fireman Mister?"

"It's Larry and yes I did used to be one son. I'm a teacher now, it's my first day. How did you know I used to be a fireman? What's your name?" Larry held out his hand expectantly.

"Dennis." Dennis shook Larry's hand gently. "Saw your picture in the paper." He snivelled and wiped his nose on his sleeve.

"So what has got you so upset Dennis?"

"Well Mist..Larry sir, it's my first day too and I don't have any friends or know anybody here!"

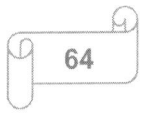

"Well you do now son – we're both in the same boat."

"But I'm not sure that I will fit in with all the other children Mr Larry sir!"

"No need to be anxious lad, you can't do everything at once. You have to do things little by little, take it nice and slow but steady – soon you'll be making friends in no time. Be like water and just go with the flow!"

Dennis started to cheer up considerably.

"Did you learn that when you were a fireman Mr Larry sir?"

"Nope, I learnt it from watching Bruce Lee films – I also found out a thing or two about kicking down doors in burning buildings!"

Dennis chuckled. "So why did you want to become a teacher Mr Larry sir?"

"Because I couldn't be a fireman anymore, son. I've been on the business end of one too many fires and it's been bad for my health. I want to spend more time with my family. I still want to help people though, which lead me to choosing to become a teacher. We have to treat change as our friend rather than our enemy Dennis. You want to be accepted by the people in school? It's about being a good friend to them and being willing to embrace change, you do both of those things and people will come to you.

"I think you will make a great teacher Mr Larry sir."

"Thanks son. You know, I have a daughter about your age and I'm sure she would like to make new friends too."

"I'd like that very much Mr Larry sir!"

*So much for chasing them away from Monique…*Larry thought.

And with that, the bell rang and they headed into class.

Give The Lad An Oscar

Oscar glanced at the snorting horse, its mad eyes terrifying, ablaze.

It was heading straight for him.

He blinked and rubbed his eyes. Could he be imagining it? Was this some kind of ghostly mirage?

No.

It was thundering towards him with the speed of a runaway freight train.

"What can I do?" He trembled to himself. He had never experienced fear like this before, raw, deep, his leg tremoring and spasming as adrenaline jolts bolted down into his overstimulated legs, freezing them until they felt filled with concrete.

"I could try to run but my legs just won't move, they're glued to the spot."

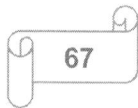

He felt like he was in a dream world – nowhere to hide, all he could do was crouch in a fetal position, cowering in anticipation, hoping for a miracle.

The beast beared down on him, closing in, all hooves and teeth and legs, hundreds of legs. Oscar hugged himself, bracing for the worse.

And then in an instant, the horse was gone, galloping past him, a gradually fading silhouette against the horizon.

Oscar gulped. *"That was close, almost too close."*

He got up and was startled to see something else. He could just about make it out in the fog. He hadn't seen him for several days but now he could clearly make him out.

His brother.

Oscar's heart skipped several beats.

"Oh brother, where art thou?" He whispered.

His brother was a playful sort, mimicking his every movement. Oscar reached out to touch his hand and it felt cold, clammy, his stare glassy-eyed but focused intently on Oscar.

His brother never said anything, always remaining silent, withdrawn, passive.

"So this is what loneliness must feel like" Oscar pondered.

Suddenly one of the big giants in the room yelled at him.

"Stop staring at that Oscar! It's broken again, staring at it won't fix it!"

"Silly old woman thought Oscar, how cruel it is to keep my brother in a box."

I'll keep watching and maybe one day I will be able to set him free when she's not looking – these giant people can't watch us all of the time.

Oscar smiled and his brother smiled back at him. *"I'll save you buddy, just you wait and see."*

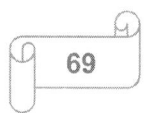

A Little Bit Of What You Fancy - A Short Story Collection

Losing The Plot

It was finally the big day of lot number #56 at the local Land & Property auction.

This was a prime piece of real estate left behind by a lonely old spinster with too many cats (and no beneficiaries either, she'd been too batty to even leave the premises to them, them kitties didn't get a sausage). This land was such a magnificent patch, it had attracted a lot of rich investors, all with specific agendas.

Mr Featherstone (slightly balding, puffy eyes, beaked nose) wanted to construct a private hospital to satisfy the hypochondriacal tendencies of his wife.

Mr Motley (spinach chin beard, impossibly long legs, fond of gold rings and other ugly male jewellery) desired a decent space to develop a block of flats.

Mr Collura (slightly sleazy, puffing a cigar, a big shot) was keen to establish both a casino and Gentleman's Club because he wanted to be famous like that Stringcheesefellow.

Mrs Crawford (snooty, glass of Pimms, a touch of hoity-toityness) – fancied turning the area into a petting zoo or a conservation park.

Mr Featherstone noticed a young girl playing with her hair and looking wistfully at the area, sadness framing her freckly face.

"Why so sad little one?"

"I want to buy the land but I only have a penny."

She shuffled awkwardly on her feet and sniffed.

"OK then Missie…"

"M'not Missie. I'm Mindy."

"OK then Mindy – if you can tell me what you will do with the land for a penny and it's better than any of our ideas then I'll buy it for you and sell it to you for that shiny penny!"

Mindy wrinkled her nose for a few seconds, whilst stroking her chin.

"I would like to build…"

"Yes, spit it out young urchin?"

"A prison."

Mrs Crawford gasped theatrically and spilled some of the ice out of her Pimms glass. The other buyers also couldn't believe their ears.

"A prison, child?"

Mindy looked defiant.

"Yes. One of them with the bars and everythin'."

"Aren't you a little young to know about those kinds of places?"

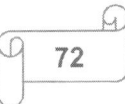

"No, my parents used to take me to one all the time. They even left me there for the day."

"How ghastly for you my dear!"

"I wasn't the only one there, it was the same for many other families with kids like me but we all got to go into the yard at lunchtime." Mindy folded her arms.

"With all of the other criminals?" Mrs Crawford squeaked in horror. "Good heavens!"

All of the buyers were now beginning to become more and more alarmed at how nonchalant Mindy was being over the whole situation.

"But why would you go to a prison child?"

"To learn things Miss."

"Seems like a rather extreme lesson to be learning at your age!"

Mr Featherstone seemed to twig at this point.

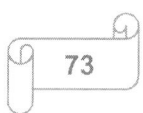

"You don't mean a prison, do you Mindy – you mean a school?"

"Ummm,….yes Mister…" Mindy bit her lip "…but it's like going to a prison."

"So why are you so upset?"

"Our school burnt down and now they are sad because there is nowhere to build a new one. If I told them I was here trying to buy a new spot for a penny they would think that I really had lost the plot!"

Mindy didn't get to spend her penny that day.

Her new-found friends however clubbed together and built her a brand new school anyway, on another patch of land close to where the original one perished.

When the school re-opened to the public, many parents remarked at how beautiful the building was and that it must have cost many a pretty penny and the teachers simply replied "No, not many, just Mindy's!"

A Little Bit Of What You Fancy

"I'm the best she'll never have!" Mr Scotchy Egg wailed, spraying pork crumbs everywhere.

"Don't take it so hard my boy, it happens to the best of us. When she's on a diet, she doesn't take any prisoners!"

"That's alright for you to say, Mr Grilled Chicken in a deliciously low fat white wine flavoured sauce but you do the vertical mambo with her a couple of times a week!"

Mr Grilled Chicken admired his perfect sculpted form in the fridge mirror.

"I admit that she has good taste and I'm in really good shape, there is hardly an ounce of fat on me at all but we're all made different, we all have our own particular appealing qualities. You for example my friend are in the Finest Food range after all."

"That's just a label, a box they put me in, it doesn't really define who I am, I'm not sexy at all, I know I taste good but I don't particularly look good." Mr Scotchy wiped a perspiratory tear from his packet.

Ms Spaghetti & Meatballs pulled the strands out of her eyes. "You think you're bad Scotchy – look at my split ends, no-one is going to fancy this!"

Mr Grilled Chicken looked at her appraisingly, with much fondness and a twinkle in his eye.

"Ms Spaghetti, my Italian love, there is no way that anyone could simply not fancy you any day of the week!"

Ms Spaghetti blushed the colour of light parmesan and shook her soft curls, sending peppered dandruff everywhere.

"How saucy Mr Grilled Chicken!"

"You'd better believe it Bella Donna!"

"Jeez you two, why don't you get a hotel room!" Mr Scotchy Egg looked on at them enviously.

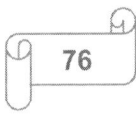

Ms Spaghetti & Meatballs frowned. "There's only one other room in this motel and the air conditioning is broken – we would freeze to death! They never seem keen to fix it…"

Suddenly a door slammed out in the netherworld and noises punctuated the door, startling them in their tracks.

"Is it our gracious queen?" Mr Scotchy whispered, looking hopeful.

Mr Grilled Chicken craned his head. "I think it is her but she has company, who could it be?"

They all kept quiet and still until they heard the giant voice speak.

"You got anything to eat Tracy? I'm famished."

"I think I have a scotch egg in the fridge."

Mr Scotchy Egg could scarcely contain his eggcitement.

"I came to the party looking to leave with the prom queen but I got her best friend instead! See you on the other side guys!"

A light blinded them for a second and then he was gone.

Mr Grilled Chicken watched him go wistfully – "I'm glad he made it, he only had one more day left and he would have had an appointment with the big, black, silvery thing outside – no-one gets out of there alive!"

Ms Spaghetti & Meatballs looked into Mr Grilled Chicken's eyes.

"Just you and me then honey?" She smiled and twirled herself around seductively.

"Should be – it's Saturday today and she doesn't do the weekly shop until tomorrow."

They cuddled up together and dreamed every meal's dream of being offered up on a smorgasbord platter with five types of cheese and wine by the bucketload. A world where 'Diets' were the name of an unpopular British folk duo band from the sixties that no-one cared to listen to.

    A bottle of champagne cheekily bubbled up next to them.

    "Here's to making new friends tomorrow – I heard on the grapevine she is going to have a naughty day and get some chocolate cake!"

They all sighed in contentment – it was the naughty days that really made life worth living.

A Little Bit Of What You Fancy - A Short Story Collection

Our Utopia

You never really appreciate something until it's gone. People always say this phrase and you never pay it much mind, until you're on the receiving end. Until you're on the other end of the baton, being generously given your reward.

Things could be worse I guess.

Seeing this world through the eyes of a child springs to mind.

First it was one at a time. Then they started rounding us up in groups. From time to time, the old, sick and the pregnant found their way into our ranks. There was little opportunity to develop relationships.

None of them lasted very long. None of them except this one.

She was young, strong, determined, a feisty character. She told me she was six months into her pregnancy when they kidnapped her and brought her here. Twice she got violently sick but somehow she managed to pull through, her resolve concrete, her will to live resolute and her determination unwavering to give life to her unborn child. We waited on tenterhooks; she missed her due date by a full week.

    Then a miracle happened.

    She gave birth.

It was a shock to see them do it here, with no medical facilities but needs must when the devil drives. The terrifying thing for us all is that the destination her child is headed to is completely unknown. Her mother hopes that one day her little daughter may be loved, will make it through this, will be cherished and can find a better life.

Will she be offered up to the faceless Gods that rule over us? Or will she be cast aside like an imperfect stone?

Only time will tell.

But for now, we get our hour of sunshine, its sweet warmth caressing away the aches, pains and crushing tiredness of the toilsome labour of the day. And we get our bowl of gruel, lovingly prepared in the community slop bucket. Maybe some things are not as bad as they seem. At least, not until the anointed hour anyway.

Then anything goes.

Then anything is better than this place.

A Little Bit Of What You Fancy - A Short Story Collection

Think Before Choosing Pink

At an abandoned subway station enshrouded in an air of desperation, dank darkness and possibly even rotting meat, Candice glanced at her watch nervously, waiting for nightfall to cloak her nefarious deal.

Candice did not have a need for money, now that she had successfully murdered her fifth husband and got away with it. She already had put her seventh child through college and had enough filthy lucre left over to buy a speedboat (a black one, with skulls, she had a thing for bikers. Who liked fishing).

The train approached but her rendezvous target was not on it. This perturbed her greatly, he had promised he would be there on the 8:08pm train, right after he had put his Mother to bed.

Puzzled, she bent down momentarily to take the pressure off her aching bunions when suddenly, out of nowhere, a bike messenger popped in, scaring her witless and dropped off a note to her.

After shaking her fist at his disappearing silhouette for several minutes, she unfolded the piece of paper and swallowing nervously, started to read.

Mouthing the words in abject horror, she began shrieking uncontrollably, screwed up the paper, hurling it in livid disgust and then hurled herself in the path of an oncoming train. The note, in its perpetuity had simply read:-

"Sorry I can't be there to finalise the 'paperwork', it's hard to get one of these through the books. I can't get you one in black too, so it will have to be in pink, OK? I think the skulls make it look kind of cute. Can we meet Friday instead? Call me. Jerry."

And to this day, this ghastly abomination sits cursed at Pier 34, waiting for an owner to claim her, an owner that will never come.

Remember – think when selecting pink – not all ladies want it.

Traditional Reservations

"The role of a woman is not limited to remaining inside her home!" Anpaytoo grumbled.

She glared despondently into the cooking pot.

"I am his other half, I make him whole, I should be out there with him!"

"Hush now Anpaytoo." Enapay the Brave, her father, sat cross legged meditating and waved his hand dismissively.

"But father, he has been gone for hours, what has become of him? Why will you not allow me to go to him? I am strong, capable, a warrior and a dedicated wife!"

Enapay chuckled.

"You are many things and have many talents my child. But you are also what the Sioux's call 'Teetonka' – you talk too much about this. He was named Akecheta by his father because he is a great fighter. He can look after himself among the wasichu, the white man. Help your noble Akecheta by being a good wife to him, he will return soon, triumphantly bestowing pride upon our great tribe."

Anpaytoo petulantly bit her lip and stroked the locket that had been given to her by Akecheta as a token of his affection. He had acquired it off an Englishman, in exchange for his own hard labour.

Akecheta told her he had worked for many weeks to afford it, such trinkets being hard to come by for their self-sufficient tribe.

"I must go and see him now!" Anpaytoo jumped up and headed for the door.

"Sit down Anpaytoo! Respect your elders, wait patiently for your husband and follow the Lakota ways."

Enapay glared at her and she shrank back into her seat like a wilting flower.

Had Anpaytoo stepped out of the tepee at that precise moment, she would have noticed the amber bracelet she exchanged with Akecheta at their wedding ceremony floating ominously down the communal river.

The bracelet was then swiftly followed by an ornate dagger, the markings on which were distinctly English in origin.

The river ran pearly pale pink for a few moments, just like the carnation Anpaytoo wore in her soft, delicate hair then it ran clear again and the dagger was gone.

"I miss him so much." Anpaytoo stroked her belly thoughtfully. "Yet I feel he will always be here with me."

"He will be here soon child, have a little faith."

"Father, you know best I guess. This is the tribal way. I will wait for an eternity if I have to."

He nodded sagely and smiled "The Lakota way."

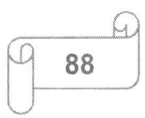

They didn't have to wait an eternity for Akecheta to enter their lives again but by then time had healed past wounds and revenge was the last thing on their minds.

"What should we call him Father?"

"Takoda would be perfect child, for one side must always show peace and compassion, despite the past. He will make good friends and form strong alliances."

Things would never be the same in their world but tradition would see them through.

Tradition is everything, especially when it comes to family.

A Little Bit Of What You Fancy - A Short Story Collection

Dodging The Issue

It's drizzling outside. A window is open and the breeze wafts in to smother me with the scent, not of a woman at all, not today, which is unusual to say the least. The clammy air tastes of dog. Funny that because I own a cat. There is a note on the wall.

Someone is trying to tell me something. A conundrum. Bringing to my attention this hum-drum existence and how I deal with this before it gets cold.

Why did I take this job? All those friends that I lost. They said the money would be good. Money can rent happiness for a while but only if you put it to good use.

My fingers hurt. Sterlize them in this whiskey. Not like I am going anywhere. Not this time. How are you supposed to learn a lesson when the only lesson to learn is that charity begins at home. That's hardly a puzzle that needs its own section in the Sunday paper.

And yet. Still. I'm unsure why. Why it happened. Forgive me, I'm all over the shop. She was too. Biting and snarling and slapping, like the devil possessed.

Bargaining chips don't come easy in an oppressive relationship. They float towards you and you grab whatever you can lay your hands on.

I think I'll sit here quietly now. Peaceful, serene. Sit on my hands until they go numb. Although I can't really feel anything now. It's been that way for a long time now. Long before we even got together.

I remember how we used to laugh and reminisce. It's all a big, swirly whirlpool now. She did leave me with something though. A little present to complement all the whiskey and tears. Her note.

I always used to tell her that her penmanship was atrocious but that usually fell on deaf ears. Now it's the thing that I treasure the dearest about her. I often used to tell her – if you write a thank you note that is crafted elegantly, you will make a deeper impression.

I turned her note over again and again but nothing more could be found.

Because in the end she wrote "Thanks for nothing."

I gave her everything, my heart, soul and being. I just couldn't give her children. They would have expected something in return.

And that's hardly a puzzle worth considering.

A Little Bit Of What You Fancy - A Short Story Collection

Give Peace A Chance

A war of voices inside my head.

Marching up and down, spinning their batons, trying to make me take notice, preening peacocks in the pursuance of fragile moments from the past, attacking with no mercy and leaving in their wake exposed raw emotion.

The pressure is getting too much, I fear I may shatter all at once, cheap glass with nothing to show for it, savour the pieces of good intentions and best laid plans.

This head that I clutch has been through a lot, a miscarriage, a failed business, an acrimonious divorce but I have always held myself with gentle grace and courage.

Grass beneath my feet feels so cool, wet and comforting in this disparate heat, it brushes against my tender arches, making me tingle and sigh, a release valve forged from nature itself.

A Little Bit Of What You Fancy - A Short Story Collection

I will not listen to their criticism, I am better than them, they will not turn me against myself, for if left unchecked, we are our own worst enemy.

The only cure for this war is peace through confidence.

A Little Bit Of What You Fancy - A Short Story Collection

A Family Of Marionettes

You know that feeling when your mouth runs away with you? That there's another entity piloting the mothership and all you can do is simply go along for the ride? Well, that happens to me all the time.

I try to apply a filter, shut off what shouldn't be there, in an unforgiving and viciously scrutinising society where one false step can be make or break in an industrious career. There's something or someone living vicariously through me, taking liberties at my own expense, with no cares in the world and he's got no brakes.

I once tried to cut him off, give him a season pass to a show at the bottom of a bottle but he rose up again, a phoenix from the dregs, dusting himself off and putting himself back as the centre of attention.

It would appear that he cannot be killed by conventional weapons, a vampire leeching off of my soul with no agenda other than to show that I'm an off kilter roller coaster with no disregard for my own goals.

My father once trod this very same path, when he too couldn't contain himself. Always making a spectacle of himself until he literally became the spectre of himself, after ruffling far too many of the wrong feathers in the seedier side of town.

He owed money to the wrong people, the kind of guys where if you shook hands with them, you would check to see if you still had your fingers. My Dad racked up massive debts and to be honest, was it any wonder when the question was asked about how difficult it would be to pick up your teeth with broken fingers what the answer would be?

This was not a rhetorical question, he soon found himself sinking to the bottom of a bottle and never managed to find his way back.

Now it would appear that the apple does not fall very far from the tree. I've mixed myself up with the very same people. Perhaps I can talk my way out of this? My own problem is I've insulted all of their Mothers and you don't do that with Italians.

It is very much a case of "Cheque, please!" but I fear that paying the bill will be the least of my worries.

When pulling the strings, be careful what you say or you may live to regret it. I started out wanting to be a star but a war of words has turned this dummy into a family of marionettes.

Pass me the bottle, I've got a feeling that this isn't going to be a long night.

A Little Bit Of What You Fancy - A Short Story Collection

Fiddling While Rome Burns To A Different Tune

A dulcet ringing in my ears, rattling for attention. The tune's fortune now tragically faded, a shadow of its former self, metallic, scratchy, a fly in a bottle trying to frantically smash its way out.

There was once an echo of such refinement and carefully composed elegance that heads would have turned instantly, a beat to cha cha and tango in time all night to, without hesitation or trepidation.

I would get entangled in it, immersed so deeply, losing myself to the steady, incessant, intoxicating rhythm, a perfect moment of blissful, aural serenity.

When the walls come crashing down though, there is little left to hold the flood back, it finds its way into all of the nooks and crannies, permeating everything that stand in its wake.

A Little Bit Of What You Fancy - A Short Story Collection

Sound, like taste and smell, can evoke powerful memories of the past, building bridges and making connections that often would better remain buried at the crossroads of time immortal.

Speaking of taste, I can only savour wetness on my tongue and it is far from pleasant. Hot, thick and unrelenting, I could whine for wine but this is a bitter claret and not one for this sensitive palate at all. I try to force it back but I am powerless to resist its unsettling warmth.

You always loved that music box, perhaps more so than me but then we both know that aural delights are what brought us together in the first place. The irony is not lost on me, as I gaze at the broken pieces that lay around me.

I hope that your new one gives you as much pleasure in the few hours that you have left. Did I mention about the poison you just imbibed in your drink? I'm sorry but I figured something was amiss and it always pays to think ahead, I just wish that I'd had the foresight to wear a helmet.

A Little Bit Of What You Fancy - A Short Story Collection

We've reached the crescendo now, everything is going grey and sombre, quietly fading out, I guess you could say they are playing our song and now they are playing for keepssss…

A Little Bit Of What You Fancy - A Short Story Collection

A Ghost Of A Chance

"Don't sit there!"

The old crone gazes at me with her one glass eyeball bulging as if it is going to burst out of its errant socket and shatter like a Christmas bauble. Her stubbly, raspy chin threatens to set fire to the well-worn rug at her feet, as she strokes her bony finger across it absent-mindedly.

I sip my lukewarm tea and cannot help but wince – these herbs have long gone off and I'm lamenting even coming here in the first place.

A friend had told me she was always right on the money and he had won the lottery last week right after seeing her. Pity he got struck by lightning three days later. Act of God they said but in my mind I thought "Easy come, easy go."

What was I hoping to get from this meeting though?

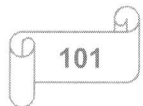

I've been unlucky in love all of my life and the thought of online dating brings me out in hives – I never know what to say or what to do, I've been winked out of existence but no-one has bothered to take it any further than that.

I carefully acknowledge the wizened old hag intently as she speaks in an eerily dull, monotonic voice.

"'E shall be 'ere soon, see deary? And when 'e comes we shall know everything there is to know about your life and your problems and we will solve them we shall, together! Bwahahahahahahaha!"

She's obviously a loon. I sincerely hope it is not because she drinks too much of this foul brew that she doles out to her customers. She probably doesn't get much in the way of repeat business.

A Little Bit Of What You Fancy - A Short Story Collection

The hairs on the nape of my neck prickle in anticipation. Who is this character she is referring to, is it a ghost, a ghoulish, ghastly apparition? There has been no sign of another human being for several minutes now and all I can think about is her introducing me to her Ouija board as a faint dampness permeates in the air.

"Come forth stranger, shower us with your knowledge and wisdom of the ages!"

I stare at her quizzically for another couple of minutes. Then wham! I'm struck full in the chest, what on earth is going on? There is dampness in the air and it is electrifying. Right up until a furry tail hits me square in the face.

I mutter in disgust, heading rapidly out of the tent and immediately boot up my laptop in my motor outside whilst mopping my face.

At least if I go back online again now, I will have the ghost of a chance of finding somebody. Even if it is only a new pet.

A Little Bit Of What You Fancy - A Short Story Collection

Part 2 - Right In The Shorts!

A Little Bit Of What You Fancy - A Short Story Collection

<u>Cherry Picking The Winner</u>

"Time to put your money where your mouth is".

I first played the odds with my childhood sweetheart, Angelina. I figured her to be a dead cert. We had big easy laughs over the most insignificant matters; the chemistry between us was raw, real and effortless. The only thing that I had to win in our relationship was her heart and I had already won that when we first rolled eyes at each other, slot machines spinning together in perfect harmony. She was the heist of the century, Oceans 11, 12 and 13 all in one go, a feisty little Madam giving me a real run for my money.

When she accepted my marriage proposal, I knew I had hit the jackpot. We got married when we both hit twenty-one (it might have been twenty-two but I'll always remember it as twenty-one, Blackjack!)

We found ourselves being hitched in a classy shindig in Vegas, with all the trimmings – swimming pool, cocktails, jacuzzi, the works and it was the happiest time of our lives.

There was trouble in our perfect little world though. The dice were always loaded from the beginning and not in my favour.

It all started to unravel one day, as if we were both pulling an irksome thread out of a sweater.

Angelina was late for work, I was taking care of 'business', there were arguments, harsh words were dealt out, nothing was black and white any more, all we could see was red and then she was gone.

I wrote her letters. Pages and pages of them. Heartfelt. Pleading. Every day begging her to come back to me. To give me another chance. She was adamant.

She said that we had reached a crossroads in our lives. That she couldn't bear to bring a child into the world we now inhabited. We all bear crosses at some point and this one had become far too big a blot on our landscape to ignore, so she had taken the high road.

For a High Roller like me, I sunk deep into dark, unfathomable, unquenchable lows that no amount of martinis could fix. My recovery took me a hell of a long time but eventually I got back in the game. No-one could ever call me a quitter, that's for sure.

My next venture had an element of international exposure, a dangerous liaison. Her name was Brigitte. Tall, elegant, sophisticated, exquisite. A German blonde who sent shivers down my spine. She had her own line of perfumes and smelt intoxicating. We met in an airport lounge bar and something clicked instantly, despite her broken English. I took a huge wager on the language barrier and in the beginning that didn't matter.

We went to beer festivals, music festivals, carnivals, Christmas markets and other wondrous places, all centred around her native homeland in Germany. Our lives were coloured, enriched, vibrant, off the charts, we were on track for the adventure of our lives. We didn't need a bucket list like most people, we were living our dreams to the fullest. I could see this particular relationship going the distance. Or so I thought.

She was a strong one, a real tough cookie, not a walkover at all. She knew exactly what she wanted and decided that I couldn't be the one to give it to her. We didn't need a steward's enquiry to realise that this filly had started to drift further and further away from me across the board until we were spread far too thin. I should have seen it coming. I'd made some bad 'business' decisions that were coming back to haunt me and this scared her off – where else did she think I was getting the money from to fund our luxuriant lifestyle?

Her chapter ended when she eloped with some guy at the German Oktoberfest. You want to know the most ironic thing about it all is? Oktoberfest isn't even really held all throughout October. What are the chances of that?

I had given up hope at this point. My heart was heavy, I felt handicapped. Permanently stuck at the starting gate of life, washed out with little to show for it. An Action Jackson with no real career goals. I'd had a double discard in the hand of life and this was the end. Spent. Crushed. Deadwood.

And then I met her. Francesca. All winning smiles, silver bullet personality in spades and an arsenal of moves that upped the ante considerably. A dancer who captured and dominated my heart, with my soul closely following suit.

She had caught my eye and I simply had to make a play for her. There were other suitors but she could see my determination, I was locked on, set on a path that no-one could shake me off, I was unbeatable.

And to think to this day I am still a terrible dancer but now I do it with grace and style, all thanks to her.

So, I'm raising a breakfast bowl of cherries in her honour, to my dearest Francesca. The only thing I'm folding is my newspaper, as I gaze at her breath-taking beauty and I'm checking to make sure that she feels the same way too.

If not then I'm flopping in the river with no anchor, no real purpose in life. I want us to have a real solid connection together – I ask myself, will she be my rock, my joie de vivre, my bridge to being a better man? If she can't give it to me straight that we're two of a kind, then I've got nothing and I'm out.

I may gamble on a lot of things but I can't take a gamble on love, not this time. I'm willing to give it all up for her, that's how much she means to me, I just need her to say the words.

I just hope she doesn't ask me to give up Bingo on Sundays because that's a bridge too far.

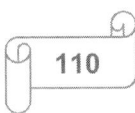

A Little Bit Of What You Fancy - A Short Story Collection

Prelude To Getting Led Out

"You don't mess with my arpeggios if you know what's good for you!"

They circled each other, eyes locked, vultures closing in on a particularly juicy carcass.

Mouths open, bodies tense with anticipation, the air crackled with discord, bending brusquely and becoming sharper, a roaring, seething mass of wailing emotions across the backdrop of an ancient Roman battleground, if ancient Roman battlegrounds were located in the market square behind Tesco.

"I laugh at your orchestral ability my dear Robert, it is lacklustre at best – you might as well pick up a stray cat and start playing it!"

Robert looked gravely at Jimmy - he had always been partial to kittens.

"What about Jazz, eh? I can play one hundred notes a minute!"

"I can knock out one hundred and fifty! Jimmy retorted.

"It takes you two whole minutes to tie your shoelaces, you liar - the song would be over by the time you managed to get the first boot on! I really don't think the ghost of Charlie Parker has got anything to worry about with you in town!"

"I'll show you where you can stick my boot in a minute Robert - I know exact which 'aria' to put it in!"

The spectacle was attracting a crowd. Some were gawping and nattering in astonishment, this glorious battle unfolding beneath their eyes like a gladiatorial soap opera, all they needed now were sopranos and tenors to give it extra panache. Or turn the whole debacle into a Go Compare Car Commercial.

Jimmy and Robert swung their guitars around their necks pointing them skyward, adopting duelling stances as if they were wielding medieval lances and were fighting for the very honour of the music maiden herself.

The odd flash went off in the background. Spoils of war for the Facebook crowd.

"Never mind rock Jimmy, you must have rocks in your head if you think that your atonal strummings sound any better than chicken scratchings on a chalkboard!"

"That's low, even for you Robert. I imagine you would have trouble keeping in time with a triangle!"

At that point, a Police Constable bobbed, weaved and conducted his way with graceful order through the throng.

"Boys, boys, boys! What do you think you're playing at?"

Jimmy & Robert looked at the Constable ashamedly, the colour rising to a crescendo in their cheeks.

Suddenly Robert gave the Constable a sideways glance and realised he was in the presence of PC Constable Doppler, a good friend of their Father.

"Hey….um…Constable Doppler is it?"

"Why yes it is son...it's Robert isn't it? I remember when you and Jimmy were wee lads, you were inseparable! Why the animosity and angry temperament towards each other?"

"It's his fault!" Jimmy pointed at Robert accusingly. "When Dad died, we couldn't keep up with the mortgage payments. We lost the house and now thanks to him, the two of us have been reduced to busking just to earn a crust!"

"You know that is a slur against my sterling character! I can't be tied down to a stuffy, 9-to-5 desk job!"

Robert drew himself up to his full not particularly impressive height of 5ft 4 inches, puffed out his chest huffily like a preening peacock and pursing his lips as if they were pursed against a very blocked tuba.

Doppler stepped in to break them up, an impromptu but necessary interval between them before their vitriolic, rhythmic reprise kicked off again.

"You both have musical talent, it seems quite obvious to me. Why don't you form a band? Your Dad always hoped that you lads would follow in the footsteps of Led Zep one day…."

"He's right - you know Robert you do have a good musical ear, probably honed from listening out for Mother to make sure that we weren't caught smoking in the garage."

"You always were highly strung Jimmy - maybe that is why I could never beat you on the mandolin."

They shook hands and then hugged. The crowd sighed in unison, a chorus of good feelings harmonising in the air.

"But what would we call ourselves?"

"Zeps Be Friends?"

Someone from the crowd piped up "Hell yeah, we'll all go!"

Three weeks later they played to a sold out show. They dedicated their performance to "The Police", which took the 'sting' out of what happened before.

Off-duty and in his civvies, PC Constable Doppler smiled at the front of the buzzing audience.

They've made their Dad proud he thought. They're calling to a different tune. He could feel a whole lot of love in the room.

He went to congratulate the boys backstage at the end of the gig and was greeted with a bickering argument.

"On the other hand…" Doppler muttered to himself "maybe it's all just a little bit of history repeating..."

Night-Bloomer

vig·i·lan·te

vigilantes, plural

Noun.

'A member of a self-appointed group of citizens who undertake law enforcement in their community without legal authority, typically because the legal agencies are thought to be inadequate.'

Dark, coffee tinged clouds roll across the sky.

This town is mine and needs saving under my watchful eye. She's a living, breathing thing. Vibrant, colourful and beautiful, in spite of the cloak of darkness that enshrouds her heavenly shoulders. I watch from the shadows, savouring the moment of anticipation like when you refrain from drinking the last drop of spirit from a glass.

A Little Bit Of What You Fancy - A Short Story Collection

The night air is cold, bitter, my breath crystallises into a myriad of honeycomb patterns. There's always a risk when you fall in love like this - the raw, naked, elemental flame of danger, coaxing seductively at your very soul. I could walk away from this at any time but she is my life, my very reason for being.

She is the anchor that I can depend upon when the world closes in on me, when I feel isolated and alone - I need her and she needs me. That is why I do this – not for the monetary reward or the recognition. I do this because I care about the town and the people more than anything in the world. I would lay my life down for this town and I'm proud of this fact.

I perform a routine check of my equipment. The tools gleam at me, razor sharp, as they bask in the incandescent glow of the moonlight. All at once I can see my purpose, my raison d'être and it too fills me with light and passion.

A Little Bit Of What You Fancy - A Short Story Collection

My town is a damsel in distress and I am her knight in shining armour, here to rescue her. Here to rescue us all.

Glancing down, I notice some nettles close to my feet in the garden where I am crouching and I carefully slip them into my carry bag pouch. They are good for medicinal purposes and have great healing properties, which will come in handy, should I encounter any resistance tonight.

I'm still waiting for the light to go off before I can make my move. It's only been a few minutes since I last gazed at my watch but it feels like I have been here for hours, I am always on tenterhooks at this stage of the operation. It's not often that a situation turns into a wearisome vigil for me but I can't afford to be careless or sloppy anymore. Not after what happened last time.

It goes without saying - fools rush in where angels fear to tread. I barely made it out of that one alive. They had weapons. They were organised. And they had an angry wasp-faced dog. I was out of action for several days afterwards and in the meantime, things were gradually turning from bad to worse.

The clement weather allowed these barbaric creatures to thrive, to multiply, to breed with a ferocious intensity, causing havoc amongst the hapless community, with no-one willing to stand up and deal with the problem.

And then there's me - the town's saviour - Incapacitated, frustrated - down and out for the count. The one man that could have made a difference and I was incapable of doing anything about it.

Until now.

My last adventure taught me a few crucially important things though. I've learnt from my mistakes.

I carry a supply of dog biscuits in my pouch to aid me, in case I have any more chance encounters with furry foes on my judicial journeys.

Time to collect my thoughts. They begin to swirl around in my head like a storm in a teacup, I try to calm them but I might as well be trying to pour warm soothing water over a raging tornado.

"How many more lives will be at stake? Who else has to suffer at the hands of this injustice? More children? Helpless animals that stray into their path? Cyclists? The list is endless!" I find myself pondering.

Suddenly the light winks off and I am startled out of my reverie, I am being called into action. I can feel the adrenaline boost thrumming away and I know I need to take this opportunity. Jumping up with alacrity, I gather my tools and I get to work. It doesn't take as long as it took last time. Suddenly the light flickers back on and I am forced to make haste.

I have barely enough time to bag my tools back up before it starts. There are angry shouts.

The sound of fear permeates the air. I hear whispers in the wind, fragments that echo and rattle along the frozen streets like runaway freight trains. Then a voice, thick and booming cuts to the chase, clear as day itself.

"Bloody vandals! What the hell does he think he's up to, interfering with my property? That's criminal damage that is!"

"I'd 'hedge my bets' that you will be causing no more trouble now with your wicked ways evil citizen!" I retort drily, with a smattering of sarcasm.

I have ascended. I'm no longer a man. And I'm not a machine either. I'm a master of the terrain, of my environment. I will always be, so long as there is fire in my belly, justice in my heart and tools on my belt. My town has been served justice well tonight - sleep well my angel.

A Little Bit Of What You Fancy - A Short Story Collection

Once again, you are now free of another crime that once tainted your fragile beauty. I'll always be there for you, as your guardian of the night. But there is always more work to be done. Evil never sleeps..........until quite late at night, as it so happens.

That is when it is time for me to shine.

That is when I bloom.

A Little Bit Of What You Fancy - A Short Story Collection

<u>Time Outside the Cage</u>

"Ooooh! Ohhh! How about these Grandma?"

Grandma Higgins squinted at her grandson Tommy in the pet store, who was now bouncing around on pogo stick legs that belied an unnatural energy, even for a seven year old. She polished her glasses and then dusted off a well-worn sigh often brought out for these kinds of occasions.

"I don't think so Tommy. Fish are such boring creatures. All blank stares, no emotion, no feeling. Kind of like my ex-husband. I mean your Grandfather."

"But they have such pretty colours! Look at how funny they do their swimming!" Tommy gushed, pressing his nose up against the glass, misting it up and causing several dozy fish to smash into his breath. "Some of them go backwards!"

"Hush now Tommy, I would only want them if they were wrapped in newspaper, served with chips and a squirt of vinegar."

Grandma Higgins huffed, whilst rooting around in her Prada handbag for a tissue to mop up the drool emanating from Tommy's gurgling lips. Tommy squirmed as she wiped the spittle off his chin - she attacked him with the deranged fervour of a particularly vigorous window cleaner being paid by the job and not the hour.

"Mummy won't let us have fish in the house because she is Al-hers-gic to them, they make her come out in lots of spots."

"A rash dear, your Mother gets a rash."

Tommy screwed up his face in concentration. "Who's she crashing into Grandma?"

"Never mind Tommy. Good grief."

Grandma Higgins circled the hutches with barely contained contempt flickering around her lips.

"How about a wittle puddy cat Grandma?" Tommy tickled his finger at a cute brown kitten that had taken a shine to him, giving him a gentle nuzzle.

"Don't speak in that way Tommy, you're nearly eight years old – it makes you sound childish."

"I'm only seven and a half; I'm still a child Grandma."

She was about to admonish him again when Tommy's attention span zinged off to another cage full of wonder and excitement.

"Oooohhhohohhhhooo - these hamsters look like fun, fun fun!"

Grandma Higgins sniffed apprehensively at them then turned her nose up snootily.

"They don't tend to live for too long dear - I prefer for a pet to have a longer lifespan than a mobile phone contract."

"Can I have a mobile phone Grandma?"

"You're too young to have one now but you'll get one some day Tommy, when you're a hotshot lawyer with all of the ladies chasing you!" Grandma Huggins winked at him conspiratorially.

"You mean girls? Ugh! No way Grandma! They smell funny and play with Barbies."

"Barbies…." Grandma Higgins looked wistful. "I used to like Ken."

"Who's Ken? Isn't my Grandpa called Derek?"

Grandma Higgins looked up from her feet, as if she were reluctantly pulling herself back from a clingy memory in her past. "It doesn't matter Tommy, anyway it's almost time for us to go."

"But you haven't chosen anything Grandma. You promised you would this time. Mummy said this is the third year now. She said you have to let go. What does she mean Grandma?"

A tear welled up in Grandma's eye that she quickly flicked away, hitting a nearby parrot making it extremely agitated and it muttered an expletive at her.

"Well I never!" She gasped, horrified indignation playing across her astonished lips. "I certainly won't be taking you home, your previous owner must have either been a pirate or a dock worker!"

The store owner came wandering over, intrigued by all of the ruckus.

"Can I help you with anything Madam?"

Tommy grabbed the owner's leg, nearly causing him to crash through a nearby display of dog whistles.

"Help Grandma to choose a fun pet Mister!" Tommy's excitement meter was threatening to go into overdrive.

"Most customers desire cats or dogs - are they not of any interest to you Madam?"

"It's Ms Higgins young man. And as for cats - their hairs get everywhere. Selfish. Always what they want - take, take, take. Dogs on the other hand…"

She paused to poke her tongue out momentarily at the owner.

"Bleu! Doing their mess all over the place. Unhygienic slobber monkeys, requiring constant attention, just like this one." She looked down at Tommy, who gave a cheeky grin, as if on cue.

"What about the rodent pet types like gerbils, hamsters or even mice Ms Higgins?"

"Certainly not, I abhor anything rodent like - that's why I divorced my husband!"

The owner thought she was joking, until a swift glance in his direction split his mirth in half like a watermelon.

Tommy started getting animated and the human space-hopper routine was being played out again, in order to get attention from the grown-ups.

"Grandma had an 'Alley-e-ghay-tor' before Mister, that's why she finds it hard to choose a pet. I want her to choose something, so I can play with it and love it and cuddle it, it will be my best friend."

The owner arched his eyebrows. "You had a croc?"

Grandma Higgins gave him a withering, condescending look as if to imply that there was nothing wrong with having an animal for a pet that was essentially a walking Louis Vuitton bag with claws and teeth.

"We live on a farm. My ex-husband got him for a snap." She snared the gaze of the owner again, who laughed, perhaps a little too nervously.

"Well if it's reptilian you're after, how about a tortoise? I'm sure your grandson would be able to handle him."

"Ohhhhohhooooo yes Grandma!" Tommy was grateful for the attention again. "Canwecanwecanwecaneplleeeeaaaase?"

At that moment, Grandma Higgins decided that enough was enough. She had to give up on the memory of 'Captain Croc'. Derek had swiped him in the divorce settlement, it really was time to move on.

"I'll take him young man!" She pointed at a tortoise, who immediately ducked into his shell.

Another similarity to my ex-husband she thought but one she could ultimately live with.

A Little Bit Of What You Fancy - A Short Story Collection

A Magical Tale Of 'The Dazzling Davido'

I'm 'The Dazzling Davido', Dynamic Daredevil of Mystery, Intrigue, Deception and Illusion.

Possibly you have heard of me but not over here I would imagine - I'm big in Japan.

You might say that at times I'm a word magician; I conjure up fabulous, fantastical stories with my prestidigitation, blurring the boundaries between fact and fiction. My sole purpose is to entertain, challenge and on occasion even frighten! I enjoy painting and crafting a vivid, lucid, vibrant world that could easily alter with a twinkle or blink of an eye. Sleight of hand for the mind.

Magic exists all around us in many different forms. Some deem it to be inspiration, rather than a divine purpose or a supernatural being; all you have to do when attending my shows is keep an open mind and above all embrace the inquisitive nature of your inner child.

A Little Bit Of What You Fancy - A Short Story Collection

Often when people contemplate the realms of the Magic Circle, they think of Harry Potter, David Blaine, Derren Brown, Dynamo, Harry Houdini and David Copperfield. I'm all these great mystical, talented men and yet I'm none of them. I'm an illusionist, an enigma; I exist simultaneously in the past, present and future.

My father once told me that "You can fool some of the people some of the time but you can't fool all of the people all of the time." Not so.

It isn't a question of hoodwinking people or pulling the wool over their eyes. It's about belief in the individual, however unpredictable, along with their level of skill. I take my duties very seriously; I'm an impeccable professional. I treat my craft as if I were a prestigious surgeon or even a spectacular Red Arrows aerobatic pilot. No room for error, no second chances. This is a career path fraught with dangerous lows and breath-taking highs. Woe betide anyone who thinks otherwise.

A Little Bit Of What You Fancy - A Short Story Collection

I'm bound by destiny, to succeed or to die at the hands of the audience every night; although it is a price I would gladly pay, if it means that each time I get it right

Pick a card; any card you want, just don't let me see it. Good. Now put it back. Anywhere you like. I'll tell you which one you chose. Then I'll look deep into your astonished eyes to your very core. Perhaps you will take a look inside yourself and realise the change from within. Now that's real magic.

I can show you a world that isn't there, what lies beneath, what exists on the periphery of your vision, what dwells deep within the recesses of your mind and imagination. I weave dreams, tiptoeing in and out of your consciousness, shifting shapes and altering perceptions then I vanish in a puff of smoke.

My favourite trick is to make a bottle of champagne disappear at the end of my shows.

That always tends to go down very nicely.

A Little Bit Of What You Fancy - A Short Story Collection

A Blast From The Past

I'm changing again.

The process is gradual. A flower slowly unfolding itself like a badly wrapped parcel that's not been stuck down properly.

It's as if I've never been that man, as if I've never been those men. They stare at me, listless sometimes - ghostly little echoes. Perpetually they look happy or surprised. It seems like I am gazing into an alternate mirror world. There are fragments of memories, pieces of the puzzle. I can feel gaps. Chasms, cracks, holes in time.

Clumsily stumbling through this barren wasteland on the way to somewhere more useful throws up the occasional landmine of regret and sorrow - bitter acquaintances with axes to grind.

They would prefer attention festooned upon them, to make them the centre of my universe, for me to wallow in their childish, fruitlessly aimless games but I pay them no mind and swiftly move on.

It's all rather tragic really. How we can all start in the same place but end up in different destinations. It's like the airport of my soul has a disparity that causes me to look on while the plane departs again. Waving goodbye madly to another dearly departed friend.

What must it be like for caterpillars that turn into butterflies? Is there no pain or even any acknowledgement of what now is, what once was and what could be? They just simply exist from that specific conceptional point onwards, nothing more, nothing less.

Distilling the essence of being like fine vodka. It can be nice to get drunk on life. Riding the euphoric wave until it crashes headlong into the here and now. Black and white, fading away and then coming back in crystal sharpness.

When we're children there is not a care in the world. The Renaissance period. We wish that life worked in reverse. Like living in a different time under an assumed identity, not being able to touch it but feeling it. Feeling what it was once like to experience miracles. When things stay the same, the comfort that they can bring is immeasurable.

I try to resist sometimes but it's a case of snakes and ladders. I climb the ladders to lofty new heights of consciousness but the insidious snakes charm me - I don't fall down with them, they nurture me, coax me and send me in a new direction entirely, building me a new path. Forged in a vivid new rainbow hue, of iron, steel, concrete and resolve - a heady mixture.

No, I can never be the man of the past. He is not me. I have changed, I have evolved, I am entering a higher level of the food chain. I cannot go back – I can visit there, I can reminisce, on some fleeting moments of past, long forgotten bliss.

But I'm changing again. The transmogrified butterflies clawing at my stomach membrane, they won't let me forget the blast from the past.

And things will never be the same.

Author Note:-

Thank you for reading this Short Story Collection.

Now that you have finished and are hopefully leaving with a smile on your face, please can you support the author by leaving a review on Amazon, Goodreads and Barnes & Noble – thank you!

"All art requires is courage and the commitment to eat a lot of biscuits." **D Ellis / 2016**